Brooklyn, NY

INTERGALACTIC

MOVING DAY

A COSMIC COUNTDOWN BY

JOHN F. MALTA

On my planet the last day of every year is Intergalactic Moving Day!

And a new one blooms and shines bright in the sky

Me and my family pile into
our Space Pod

And prepare for launch!

10

I always remember to pack my robot

9

And my favorite snacks!

8

Oh! And of course my
lucky caps!

I remind Dad to pack his
glasses and our baseball gloves

6

Mom packs up her office and her book collection

5

**And her
old wrestling trophies!**

Just before take-off we all pose for one last photograph in front of our home

3

Then we buckle up

2

And hold hands as we
   prepare to celebrate...

After the stardust settles we sit back and take in the glowing glimmer of our new home planet

Intergalactic Moving Day
Text and Illustrations © 2021 John F. Malta

Published by POW!
a division of powerHouse Packaging & Supply, Inc.
32 Adams Street, Brooklyn, NY 11201-1021

www.POWKidsBooks.com
Distributed by powerHouse Books
www.powerHouseBooks.com

First edition, 2021

Library of Congress Control Number: 2021937203

ISBN 978-1-57687-995-5

Printed by Toppan Leefung

10 9 8 7 6 5 4 3 2 1

Printed and bound in China